DANIEL
AND THE
IVORY PRINCESS

Written and Illustrated

by

Kevin Martin

dp

Distinctive Publishing Corp.

Library of Congress Cataloging-in-Publication Data
Martin, Kevin, 1966 —
Daniel and the Ivory Princess
written and illustrated by Kevin Martin
    p.   cm.
Summary: When he hears that a human expedition is looking for the rare white dolphin known as the Ivory Princess, Daniel, a young dolphin, determines to save her from capture.
    ISBN 0-942963-50-4 : $14.95
    1. Dolphins—Fiction.   2. Marine animals—Fiction.
    3. Endangered species—Fiction.   I. Title
PZ7.M36336Dan   1994
[Fic]—dc20   94-34556
                                                              CIP
                                                              AC

Typesetting by Mary Bredbenner

Distinctive books are available at special discounts when purchased in bulk for premiums and sales promotions as well as for fund-raising or educational use. Special Editions or book excerpts can also be created to specification. For details, contact the Special Sales Director at the address below.

dp

DISTINCTIVE PUBLISHING CORP.
P.O. Box 17868
Plantation, Florida 33318-7868
Manufactured in the United States of America

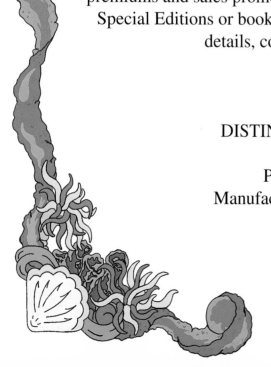

DEDICATION

For the One who gave us the dolphins below
and the stars above.

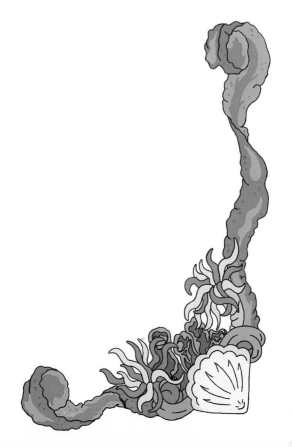

ABOUT
THE AUTHOR

Kevin Martin, an award winning artist, has always been fascinated by the behavior of dolphins. Born and raised in Illinois, Martin has used dolphins as the subject of his many paintings and sculptures. Daniel and the Ivory Princess, is the first in a series of a children's stories written and illustrated by Martin. His aquatic research and artistic background were the inspiration for this thoroughly entertaining and educational tale.

ACKNOWLEDGEMENTS

Thank you to a very special family for all your ideas and support, especially Mom and Dad for believing in me and for helping me reach for the stars, it means a great deal to me. Thanks to Pat Huss for her continuing assistance and believing in my work, while also teaching me to believe in it. To Pastor Jamie Deuser, your family and Hope Community Church (That place is contagious!) for all your faith and encouragement. To a man named Walt, for reaching higher than anyone ever has, thanks for the inspiration. Thanks to our special friends, the dolphins, lets not blow it folks. A special thanks to Laura for putting up with me, being able to decipher my writing and for being behind me through the whole crazy process. Thanks for being there. To my friends that I don't have room to mention, it's been a crazy last couple of years and I appreciate the support. To Daniel who I really haven't had a chance to meet yet, but am looking forward to the day I do. Thank you to Distinctive Publishing for giving me a chance. Most of all, an everlasting thanks to God for all of this, helping me believe in myself and for giving us all something to reach for.

CHAPTER 1

ONCE UPON A TIDE, IN A FARAWAY PLACE the fiery brilliance of the afternoon sun reflected off the calm glistening waters that hugged Daniel, a stout little dolphin, while he playfully enjoyed one of natures most beautiful possessions, the mysterious sea.

Daniel, with a heart as big as his dreams, loved soaking up the sunshine, daydreaming of one day becoming one of his heroes. Maybe being the first dolphin in space, or perhaps hitting the winning home run in the Deep Sea World Series...

Daniel continued dreaming these wonderful fantasies until suddenly from under the ocean's depths, a pudgy webbed hand broke through the peaceful surface and pulled him under.

Little Daniel would become a hero sooner than he thought, as his adventure was about to begin.

Bewildered, he breathed a sigh of relief. It was his friend Nikki, the sea otter.

"What's the big idea?" Daniel choked and sputtered. Nikki was out of breath as she exclaimed, "I've been looking all over for you Daniel, the coach needs you now!"

"Why?" Daniel pouted. "I thought the coach had enough players for the rest of the series." Daniel was a player on the Shallow League coralball team, the Aqua City Dolphins, who were playing the Salt Reef Stingers in the Shallow League Marine Series.

He wasn't a bad player, he just never seemed to get any breaks.

"That's just it Daniel," Nikki explained. "He did until Dolphy went out with a sprained fin. You're the team's only hope!

Come on Daniel, reach for the stars! Show them you can do it!

2

Daniel never had a chance to reply. Nikki grabbed him by the tail and dragged him to the game.

When they arrived, Daniel quickly suited up and swam to the plate, bat in fin he gazed at his teammates. He just couldn't let them down again. This time he would prove he could do it.

The Dolphins were down two to one in the bottom of the ninth with only one out. Daniel settled down and concentrated as the Stingers pitcher let go a pretty good fastball. Daniel swung...

3

The next thing he knew, he was standing at first base, putting his team in a position to tie the game. The crowd was still going wild as the next batter came to the plate. Daniel readied himself to race for second base. The batter hit a ground ball between first and second. Just as Daniel started to swim, the Stingers first baseman slipped his tail around Daniel's tail, tripping him on his way to second. Nobody witnessed what the first baseman had done. He then scooped up the ball, tagged Daniel, then first base. It was a double play. Game over. Daniel just hung his head. He felt awful because, once again, he messed things up.

"It's kinda hard reaching for the stars with your face in the sand," Daniel said to himself. The coach swam over to Daniel. He braced himself for what the coach was about to say.

The coach sternly looked down and said, "Don't worry about it Dan, everybody has days like this. We still have one more game left. Go home and get some rest. I'll see you back here in a couple of days and we'll get 'em then."

The coach helped Daniel up, gave him a reassuring smile, then swam away. Daniel couldn't believe it. The coach was actually going to give him another chance. Daniel felt better until he heard the other players snickering and laughing.

Nikki, floating alongside Daniel, comforted him by saying, "Don't pay any attention to them Daniel. What happened today could have happened to anyone."

"I've been hearing that a lot lately Nikki. Maybe I should just change my name to Anyone," Daniel grumbled. " I'm sorry Nikki, you're right. I'm not gonna let them get me down. I'll be back and I'll show them I'm the best player on this team or any team. I'm reaching for the stars and I'm gonna get one, you'll see!"

"That's the spirit Daniel," Nikki beamed. "And you know what? All this excitement has made me hungry.

Do you mind if we grab something to eat on the way home?"

"All right Nik," remembering sea otters had enormous

appetites, "but you'll have to eat for both of us. I'm not very hungry right now."

"If you insist, Daniel," Nikki blushed. They smiled at each other and swam home.

CHAPTER 2

DANIEL COULDN'T REST AFTER THE DAY'S excitement. He flipped and flopped all night thinking about the last game of the series. Suddenly, Daniel heard voices outside his room. He swam over to the door and peeked out. Daniel quickly realized it was the Unification of the Dolphins, a meeting held annually or in emergencies. This must have been an emergency because the next meeting wasn't due for months. Daniel's father was in charge of this meeting.

He addressed the council, "Fellow dolphins, I have called this meeting tonight because of a problem I fear affects us all. The Great Angelfish, Diviniti, has called upon us to join together. She has foreseen a human expedition that has set out to the Ivory Coast to capture the sea's most precious inhabitant, the Ivory Princess."

8

"The Ivory Princess!" a gasp went over the entire conference. Daniel couldn't believe it either. He had heard of the Ivory Princess in fairy tales and books, but no one ever actually saw her. She was said to be the most beautiful of all the dolphins, pure white and beautifully graceful. She was so special in fact, that the Ivory Coast was named after her. Daniel enthusiastically listened as his father continued.

"The Princess has been calling for help. The expedition may reach her within a couple of days."

One of the elders spoke up, "Why does man seek the Ivory Princess when so many of our kind live with them already?"

"The Ivory Princess is the last of the white dolphins, very rare and unique," Daniel's father answered. "A new aquarium is about to open and the Ivory Princess is to be the star attraction. It is true, humans and dolphins have been getting along for centuries, but sometimes people take advantage of this friendship. The Ivory Princess is the last of a very special, endangered breed. She symbolizes the gentleness and greatness of our race. You know as well as I that the Princess will not survive away from her waters."

The group looked at each other not knowing what to say.

Daniel's father said, "I believe it is up to us to protect her. We have to join together and turn this expedition away."

The elders argued the problem and finally gave their answer.

"We have come to a decision," a spokesfin said to Daniel's father. "The council members all agree, we too have families to protect and this small group of dolphins would be no match for an armed human expedition. It is too dangerous. We will have to come up with another plan." The meeting continued for hours and Daniel knew as well as his father that there wasn't enough time for another plan.

Daniel quietly swam back to his room and wrote a note to his parents. He decided he alone would save the Princess.

He would prove to everyone that he could do something special. Daniel finished his letter, grabbed his coralball cap and set out to save the Ivory Princess.

CHAPTER 3

DANIEL DECIDED TO FIRST VISIT THE Coral Castle, home of the Great Angelfish, Diviniti. She was waiting for an answer from the Unification. She also knew more about the human expedition than anyone and could probably help with directions and any other questions Daniel had about his mission.

The castle lay just beyond the clear blue waters of the Crystal Reef. Daniel spotted it in the distance, shining like a magical beacon through the water. It was as gorgeous as he had heard, a magnificent emerald coral castle surrounded by beautiful walls of glistening emerald stone. The walls enclosed a courtyard of the ocean's most beautiful flowers and plants.

Daniel entered the castle and swam directly to the throne of the Great Angelfish.

"Welcome Daniel, have you brought the Unification's answer?" Diviniti softly whispered.

At first, Daniel was surprised that she knew his name, but remembered that the Great Angelfish had special abilities.

"Well, kinda," Daniel replied.

"You're the answer, aren't you Daniel?" Diviniti chuckled.

"Huh, well you see, my dad isn't having much luck with the other dolphins, so he's working on another plan. It doesn't look good and besides, time's running out," Daniel sighed.

The Great Angelfish couldn't help being disappointed with the Dolphin Unification.

"Yes, let them debate as long as they want while the bravest of their kind goes out and shows them the way."

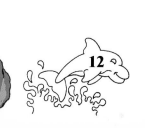

"Does that mean you think I can do it? I'm really gonna be able to save the Princess," Daniel flipped happily.

"Your pride in being a dolphin and your love for all kind will help you on this difficult mission,"

Diviniti declared. "Believe in yourself, in your dreams, and nothing will ever stop you from making them come true."

"Reach for the stars, right?" Daniel asked.

"Right Daniel," the Great Angelfish answered as she wrapped her flowing fins around Daniel. "That's what's so special about the stars, nobody can possess them. They are there to be shared by all, our friends, families, and even our enemies. Like your dreams, nobody can ever take them away," Diviniti smiled. "Keep reaching for the stars and you will be able to accomplish anything you set out to do."

"Just keep reaching, huh? You're right, Your Highness," Daniel shouted. "I'm going to reach for the highest star!"

"That's it, Daniel. You carry more courage and confidence on those brave little shoulders than you will ever know. Good luck on your journey and be sure to stay clear of Seavil."

"The Sea Dragon?" Daniel asked.

"Yes, he is nothing but trouble and is sure to interfere with this mission," the Great Angelfish warned. "His heart is unlike yours. It is black and full of evil."

"Actually I was going to visit him next," Daniel grinned.

"I have a plan that I think he could help with."

"You are one of a kind Daniel, I'm glad I had this chance to meet you," Diviniti smiled. "Be careful and good luck."

With that, Daniel was once again on his way.

CHAPTER 4

DANIEL COULDN'T LEAVE WITHOUT FIRST telling his friend
Nikki goodbye. After he explained everything, Nikki insisted on going
along. Daniel warned that it would be too dangerous, but Nikki wasn't
about to take no for an answer. Daniel was impressed by her courage and
had to admit having her along would be nice. So the twosome started out
for the Mountains of Darkness, the home of the Sea Dragon.

"You wouldn't mind if I indulge in a little traveling snack, would you
Daniel?" Nikki sheepishly asked. Daniel was grateful for her
company and knew her appetite would go wherever she went.

"Not at all, Nikki," Daniel smiled. "Just so it doesn't slow us
down."

"All right, lunch time!" Nikki squealed as she gulped down some
clams. Each time she opened a new clam with the stone she had placed
on her chest, Nikki's little belly would jiggle. That was all Daniel
could take as he burst into giggles.

"What's so funny?" Nikki gurgled.

"Nothing, just glad you're my friend. Keep swimming, Nik."

Before they reached the Mountains of Darkness, Daniel noticed a dark and scary shadow lurking below them, which meant that something equally menacing was swimming behind them. Daniel didn't look back. He swam on hoping their pursuer would swim away. The shadow did just the opposite, growing closer and closer. He couldn't take it anymore. He had to look back, but wished he hadn't. He was looking straight into the eyes of the most vicious looking shark he had ever seen. This sight gave both Daniel and Nikki a good reason to swim faster than they had ever swam before. They raced past plants and coral, around cliffs and through caves, but the shark was not letting up. They just couldn't lose him.

"Nikki," Daniel gasped, "are you still hungry?"

"Hungry?" Nikki barked. "Who can think about eating at a time like this?"

"Uh, how about that big shark behind us?" Daniel joked as he raced by. "Swim faster Nikki!"

Daniel had no problem keeping ahead of the shark, but Nikki's eating habits were starting to take their toll as she began to slow down. The shark took advantage of her decreased speed and cornered Nikki against the wall of a decaying ancient fortress.

Daniel looked back in horror. His little friend was about to become lunch for the hungry beast.

Daniel discovered the structure Nikki was trapped under wasn't stable. In fact, there was a deep crack directly above the shark's body, giving Daniel an idea.

Daniel, like other dolphins had the ability to produce certain squeaks and screeches used to track and stun food. Luckily, Daniel had a special sonic screech that was louder than others.

"Hold your ears, Nikki," Daniel shouted. "Here I come!"

Nikki did as he said. Daniel rocketed by the fragile structure, letting out his special sonic screech. It wasn't enough to stun the shark, but is was enough to rattle the cracked structure above the shark. The shock wave brought the crumbling fortress down on the shark, trapping him inches away from Nikki.

"A little screech, rattle and roll," Daniel bragged as he zipped by his shaky friend. "Got 'em on that one, huh Nik?"

"NNNNNever ddddoubted you a minute Danny,"Nikki said. "Thanks."

The two victorious friends swam on.

Daniel looked back and couldn't help but feel sorry for the helpless shark.

"Uh, Nikki," Daniel hesitantly whispered, "I know this is going to sound crazy, but we have to go back and help the shark."

"Take it easy Dan. I think that sonic screech of yours stunned you a little," Nikki joked. "It just sounded like you said you wanted to save the poor ole shark that just about had me for an appetizer and you for his main course."

"I'm not stunned Nikki. He was chasing us because he was hungry," Daniel explained. "Sharks have to eat, too. You should appreciate that. If we don't save him, he'll drown. "

Nikki couldn't believe she was doing this. She and Daniel uncovered the buried shark, who squeezed out from under the remaining rubble and gratefully shook Daniel's fin and hugged Nikki.

"My name is Karky," the shark said introducing himself. "I'm awfully sorry about the chase. Those are some pretty slick moves you have there Danny, and that screech, wow! I can't believe you guys came back to save me. It was probably your idea, wasn't it Nikki? Thanks a lot," Karky chattered, kissing Nikki on the head.

After Karky was finished showing his gratitude Daniel told him about their mission and asked if he would help.

"Look guys, it's not that I don't appreciate what you just did, but if anyone found out I was helping a dolphin and a sea otter I would be laughed at and shunned by my friends," Karky said, putting his head down.

"Yeah, well if they found out what just happened here they might find it pretty amusing. What do you think, chum breath?" Nikki barked.

"Oh you wouldn't tell anyone, would you?" Karky begged.

Daniel paced back and forth, thinking all the while.

"Not if you promise to talk to your fellow sharks and try to get them to help," Daniel said.

"Maybe changing your diet wouldn't be a bad idea either!" Nikki snapped.

"You can count on me Nik. I'll do what I can Danny. I'll never forget what you have done. Thanks again and good luck," Karky said as he disappeared into the distance.

CHAPTER 5

DANIEL AND NIKKI REACHED THE MOUNTAINS of
Darkness without anymore interruptions. The erie Home of the Sea
Dragon stood sinisterly at the lower depths of the mountains.
Guarding the entrance were the ocean's most disgusting creatures,
the seathons. Slimy and snake-like, they thrived in this part of the
ocean.   "MMMMMaybe we could come up with another plan,"
Daniel stuttered to Nikki.

The lead seathon interrupted annoyingly, "Come to see the master, have you? Need his help, do you?"

"How do you know so much about us?" Daniel questioned.

"The master knows everything, doesn't he? Waiting for you inside, isn't he? Going to make a deal with you, is he?" the seathon shrieked.

They both took a deep breath and cautiously swam into the gaping jaws. Nikki clung tightly to Daniel as they shivered through the creepy cavern.

23

When they reached the entrance to Seavil's throne-room, a thunderous voice rumbled, "Come in, I've been expecting you."

They hesitantly swam in, amazed by the enormous size of the foul smelling den. Seavil lounged repulsively in the middle of what seemed to be the biggest collection of treasure Daniel had ever seen.

Daniel spoke up, "Excuse me, Your Mightiness, I am Daniel, Daniel Dolphin and I am here with a proposal that will keep the spirit of the sea as well as its most precious inhabitant alive."

"Enough!" Seavil coldly cut Daniel off. "It is I who has a proposition for you."

"Has a favor does he?" one of the seathons squealed, sliding around Seavil's leg.

"You see," Seavil calmly continued, "long ago, my forefathers battled the ghastly moray eels over rightfully being crowned King of the Deep. This fighting went on for years. The moray's possessions never did equal the sea dragon's until one gloomy night, many years ago. The sea dragon's most prized possession, the Eye of the Dragon, a beautiful gold encrusted stone pendant more brilliant than a million stars, was taken from its resting place. To keep the sea dragons from reclaiming the pendant the morays constructed the Cave of the Serpents."

Seavil snarled as he concluded, "The entrance is only big enough for the morays and built to resist the sea dragon's might. The pendant was never recovered. Due to this outrageous stunt, the sea dragon's pride was crushed and we quickly became extinct. I alone, the Great Seavil, am what remains of a once proud and mighty race."

Seavil grimaced as he delivered his proposal, "If the Eye of the Dragon is retrieved, the honor of the sea dragon will be restored and I will once again hold my head high. You see, my little seathon cousins have tried for years to solve the cave's mysteries and secrets, but they are just not bright enough," Seavil smirked. "You two, on the other hand, look very capable indeed. What do you say?"

"If we do bring back the pendant will you help us rescue the Princess?" Daniel asked.

"I don't believe so," Seavil chuckled.

"Doesn't think so, does he? Not bright enough, are we?" The seathons shrieked.

"I will, however, return one of your most precious possessions to you in exchange for the pendant," Seavil grinned coldly.

"I don't think there's anything here that would interest me. Dolphins, unlike sea dragons, cherish life more than treasures," Daniel sneered. "Maybe that's why our race still exists, while you and your greed has brought your race to extinction. Sorry we took up so much of your time." Daniel turned to leave and Seavil laughed loudly.

"My point exactly, my brave little fool. There seems to have been a worried father who ventured off after his crazy son. Well, that same father wandered through these waters shortly before you and is now my privileged guest."

27

Daniel's fears were realized as he looked in the direction Seavil wickedly pointed. Daniel's father was held captive in Seavil's dark, dreary prison. Daniel lunged to help his father, but Nikki, knowing it would only make things worse, held him back.

The pathetic seathons joined in Seavil's revolting celebration, "Has your daddy prisoner, does he? All you have to do is return the pendant, do ye? Then everybody will be happy, will we?"

The cavern rumbled with Seavil's sinister laugh, "Get me the Eye of the Dragon and I'll let you all go."

CHAPTER 6

DANIEL AND NIKKI QUICKLY LEFT THE craziness of the sea dragon's home. Daniel had to think, and think fast since he and Nikki just inherited another rescue mission. They both headed for the surface.

Daniel broke the waves of the surface and smacked right into a rather small diver's mask containing two rather large eyes staring back at him.

"Who are you?" Daniel questioned.

"Scuba's the name," the squirrel proclaimed, brushing himself off. "Scuba the Sea Squirrel, and who are you?"

"Daniel, Daniel Dolphin and this is my friend Nikki." Nikki was slightly amused, and showed little interest as she kept eating the treats she had just gathered from the ocean's floor.

"Wait a minute," Daniel laughed, "Sea squirrel? There's no such thing as a sea squirrel!"

29

Look Daniel," Scuba insisted, there are ground squirrels, tree squirrels, and there are even flying squirrels. Why can't there be a sea squirrel? You're a mammal just like me, and you live in the water."

"Okay, I guess you're right," Daniel admitted, "but why the sea?"

Scuba, leaning against a rock, explained his desire for the sea, "A guy like me can only take so much gathering and eating nuts, living in a tree and sleeping on branches. Gets pretty boring after awhile. Now the deep...it's mysteries, dangers, beauties and especially its gorgeous treasure, that's excitement."

"Looking for treasure, are you?" Daniel smiled as he glanced at Nikki.

"Scuba's the name and treasure's my pleasure," Scuba proclaimed. "I've been itching to look for treasures ever since I designed this special scuba gear. This little number can keep me under water longer than you two. What do you say Danny Boy, know of any sunken treasure around here?"

"It just so happens my friend Nikki and I are on our way to the Cave of the Serpents," Daniel said.

"Really," Scuba replied, taking the bait.

"Yeah," Daniel teased, "which happens to contain the Eye of the Dragon, the most precious and brilliant stone in all the seas."

"Yeah, yeah," Scuba drooled.

"Yeah, and I suppose we could use an inventive fella like you, that is if you would like to come along," Daniel urged.

"I'm in," Scuba flashed a thumbs up sign.

"All right then, let's go," Daniel flipped back under the waves, explaining the entire story to Scuba on the way."

CHAPTER 7

THE TRIO APPROACHED THE CAVE OF THE Serpents, which was pretty impressive and effectively frightening. The massive monument was a marvelous reproduction of the ferocious Sea Dragon.

They all glided through the gaping mouth of the monstrous stone beast.

The caverns inside contained numerous stalagmites and stalagtites, which presented quite a challenge as the threesome twisted and turned their way through the dangerous caves.

The first tunnel they encountered had walls lined with skeletons. Each skeleton held above its head a massive ancient battle axe. Daniel figured passing by the skeletons would trigger the axes to drop on unsuspecting adventurers.

"Scuba, you're the inventive one, any suggestions?"

"Let's see, it's too shallow to go over, can't go underneath," Scuba pondered. "Okay, maybe I'm not a genius."

They all struggled for an idea. Then suddenly Nikki shouted, "I've got it!" as she raced from the room.

Scuba and Daniel looked at each other, bewildered. Nikki returned shortly after, her arms overflowing with clam shells.

"This is not a good time to eat, Nikki," Daniel growled.

"There is never a bad time to eat," Nikki pointed out. "But I'm not eating, these shells are already empty. Follow me on this one guys. One of us takes the empty shells, ties them to one of our backs, then swims under the axes. The blades will just bounce off the shells, then the other two can follow safely."

"That's brilliant, Nikki! The shells will act as armor," Daniel said excitedly.

Nikki couldn't keep from blushing happily.

"Well since my fin and Scuba's tank would get in the way, it looks like you're the one going first Nikki," Daniel said.

"I just knew you were going to say that,"Nikki squawked. "I should be eating clams, not wearing them."

"Hey Nikki," Daniel knew he had to get Nikki's mind off the challenge, "aren't those sea urchins on the other side?"

Daniel knew that sea urchins were Nikki's favorite food and before they finished securing the last shell, Nikki darted across the tunnel. With one hand over her eyes, she raced on, triggering the massive axes as she went. Her plan worked. The axes just bounced off the shells protecting her furry little body.

Upon reaching the other side, Nikki gratefully indulged in the sea urchins, celebrating her triumph. Scuba and Daniel followed, cheering all the way.

"You did it Nikki, you did it!" they both shouted. Just then the cave started to shake and rumble.

"Uh-oh," Scuba trembled, "this cave doesn't seem to be very stable. We'll have to keep it down from now on."

With this in mind, they quietly moved on.

36

CHAPTER 8

Traveling through the caverns grew more and more difficult. The deeper they swam, the darker it became. Finally visibility inside the underwater maze disappeared completely.

Daniel stopped. Scuba and Nikki crashed into Daniel.

"Hold it guys, we can't go on risking getting hurt in this darkness," Daniel said. "Both of you take hold of my tail and we'll glide through this blackness using Dolphin-vision."

"Where's your tail?" Scuba and Nikki joked.

"Let's go you two," Daniel laughed as he guided them skillfully through the dark using his dolphin sonar. The small squeaks and chirps Daniel used were just enough for him to find safe passage through the murky caves.

Finally, a faint glow appeared ahead and they were able to see again.

"The Fangs of the Serpent," Nikki informed the group as she read the inscription above the entrance.

37

They were completely puzzled as they gazed into a cavern, empty except for a small lever on the opposite wall.

Scuba picked up a small stone and hurled it across the cavern. As the stone whizzed by the holes in the wall, gigantic fangs sprang out.

"I knew it," Scuba announced. "Most, but not all of the holes in the cave contain fangs that when passed over will spring into the path of the passerby."

"Let me guess?" Daniel spoke up. "That lever on the opposite side will retract all the fangs allowing anyone to pass."

"Exactly!" Scuba agreed with a thumbs up.

Daniel figured he should take this one because he was the quickest, most agile swimmer of the three. His quick twists and sharp movements effectively dodged the fangs, which seemed to spring even faster as he swam on. Nikki and Scuba could hardly watch. The fangs shot out faster and faster with one catching Daniel off balance as he failed to turn quick enough. The fang did not get Daniel, but did pierce his cap, tearing it off his head. Daniel kept cool, and didn't lose his concentration as he raced past the remaining fangs, reaching the lever on the other side. Daniel pulled the lever down and, as expected, the fangs disappeared. Nikki and Scuba swam over to congratulate Daniel. Nikki picked up Daniel's cap on the way over and placed it, hole and all, on his brave little head.

"Good job, Daniel," Nikki said as she kissed him on the cheek.

"This is pretty fun, huh?" Scuba smiled, thumb in the air as he headed for the final challenge.

Daniel and Nikki looked at each other shaking their heads as they followed their cocky little friend.

39

CHAPTER 9

THE THREESOME SWAM ON, REACHING THE chamber that housed the Eye of the Dragon. The room was filled with glistening gold, jewels and treasures, which added to it's majesty.

Seeing the beautiful pendant made Scuba's eyes grow wider. He was hypnotized by the beauty of the pendant.

There it was. His for the taking.

40

He charged for the precious stone.

Daniel didn't like this. It was too easy. He gazed at the massive moray eel shaped pillars and the engraving of the two morays striking at the magnificent pendant.

That was it, Daniel thought as he grabbed Scuba and pulled him back seconds before a couple of vicious moray eels snapped out from behind the grate.

"Still having fun, Scuba?" Daniel smirked with a thumbs up. "I don't think the morays are just gonna let you take that pendant."

"Okay, maybe they won't when they're awake, but what about when they're sleeping?" Scuba asked. "Can you knock them out with that sonic screech of yours?"

"Well they're kinda big," Daniel answered, "but it might stun them for a little while."

"Okay, we get one of those axes back there and use it to cut through all of the bars except for the middle one." Scuba continued, "While the morays are stunned, you and Nikki swing the grate around and hold it in place. This will give me enough light to pry the pendant away from the grate. When the pendant is off, we swing the grate around, tie it down, separating us from the bad guys. Then we're outta here."

They went ahead with Scuba's plan and everything worked as planned, but the clamp holding the pendant was very rusty and it was taking Scuba longer than he thought. With a bellowing roar, the morays awoke and raced toward their newly acquired cell mates.

"Excuse me, Scuba," Daniel spoke up, "I think that sound means the morays are on the way."

"I've almost got it, hang on," Scuba pleaded.

"How about we swing this grate around and you can work on it over here," Nikki cracked.

The morays were getting closer and closer.

"Lunch time, Scuba," Daniel joked.

"I've got it!" Scuba said just as the morays were about to snap at Daniel and Nikki.

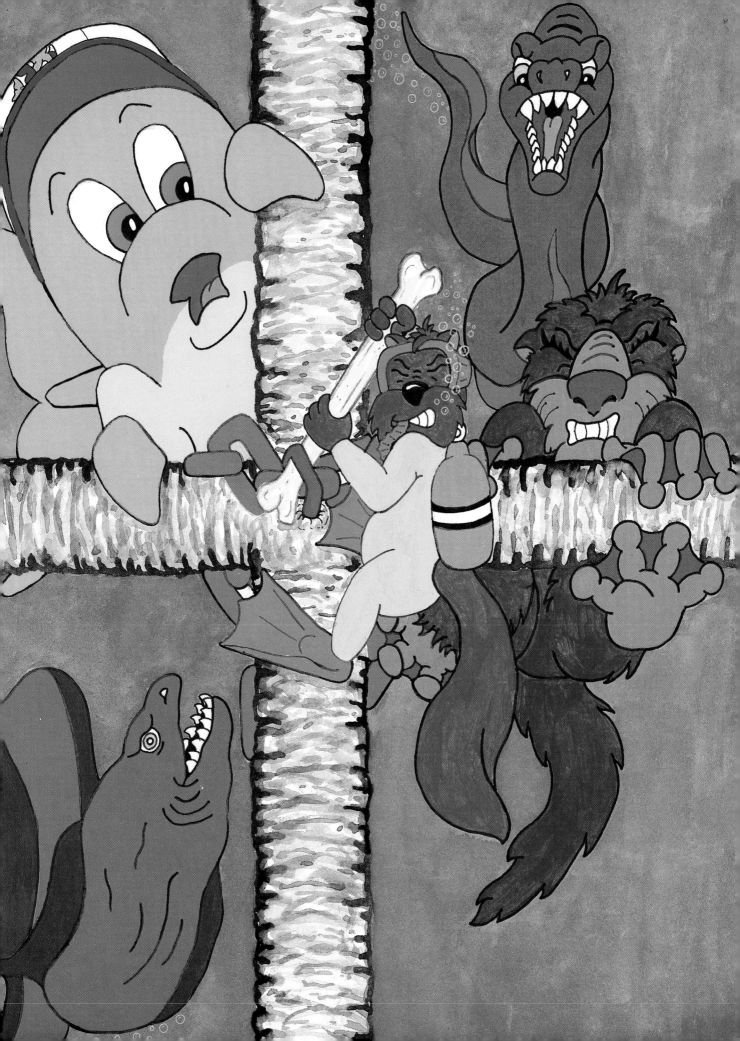

Scuba was already busy tying down the grate as Nikki and Daniel recovered from being swung back around.

"Let's go you two. Grab that crown and some treasure, we'll need it later, and let's get outta here. It won't be long before they gnaw their way through the rope," Scuba urged.

Scuba was right. In the time it took the threesome to grab some treasure and race for the entrance, the morays had already cut through the rope and were in hot pursuit. Daniel dropped back a little, while Nikki and Scuba charged forward.

"Keep going guys and make as much noise as possible!" Daniel grinned, racing along.

The cave began to buckle and shake. Daniel's idea was working but their shouting needed a little more volume. Just before they cleared the entrance, Daniel topped off his friend's shouting with another one of his sonic screeches.

The screech knocked out his little friends and brought the caves entrance crashing down, sealing in its mysteries and horrible monsters forever. Daniel held onto his unconscious friends and raced safely to the surface.

CHAPTER 10

"**S**ORRY ABOUT THAT GUYS," DANIEL shrugged, as Nikki and Scuba awoke. "I had to act quickly or we never would have made it out of that cave alive."

"That's all right Dan. We'll be fine, right Nikki?" Scuba shot up a shaky thumb. Nikki smiled and shook her spinning head.

"Okay, let's get outta here," Daniel hurried.

"Wait a minute," Scuba said. "That screech of yours gives me, besides a big headache, a very good idea. This Seavil we're going to visit is shifty and can't be trusted, right?" Scuba asked.

"Yeah, but he's too big to knock out with my screech," Daniel added.

"But if your sonic screech was amplified..." Scuba smiled. "I have a backup plan in case that sea dragon tries to back out of his promise."

"All right Scuba, what do you have in mind?" Daniel asked.

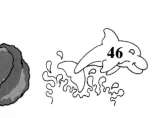

"Nikki, you're gonna like this. First, I need you to empty two of those big clams over there. Then I'm gonna have to borrow that crown you found."

Nikki wasn't too happy about losing the crown, but quickly forgot as she started eating the clams.

"Okay, this is the plan..." Scuba explained to Daniel, pulling a small tool kit from his wet suit.

Shortly after, the threesome were on their way back to visit Seavil. This time they just passed by the seathon guards. Seavil's eyes bulged as they entered.

"You did recover the pendant," Seavil hissed. "Impressive, very impressive. You little creatures are better than I thought."

"Not only did we bring back your pendant, Your Highness, but a treasure that is second in beauty only to your majesty, Great One" Daniel continued. "Seavil, King of the Deep, I present to you the Golden Crown of the Morays, a treasure that will surely restore honor to the sea dragons."

Seavil's jaw dropped as Nikki and Scuba placed the crown on his scaly head.

"Ah yes, yes. This is truly a great day for the sea dragon," Seavil squealed. "Not only is the Eye of the Dragon rightfully returned, but also the crown of our enemy, making us once again Kings of the Deep. The pendant please."

Of course, the pendant," Daniel studdered. "Once you have the pendant you will keep your promise and let my dad go, right?"

"Yes," Seavil grinned. "I'll even help you with your rescue."

"Then you'll go with us!" Daniel cheered.

"Not exactly," Seavil grimaced. "I will help by not letting you crazy little fools go up against that armed expedition. I'll keep you all safely locked up here in my spacious sea cells."

Daniel couldn't believe Seavil was backing out on them. "It looks like everybody was right about you," Daniel snapped as Seavil pulled him closer to eye level. "You're nothing but a mean, selfish, greedy old snake. You have no honor. You don't even belong in the same water with the rest of us."

Nikki and Scuba smiled. They couldn't believe Daniel was talking to Seavil like this.

"We risked our lives to bring back your precious treasure and all we asked for in return was your help." Daniel continued, "That's all right Seavil. Instead of working with us you can just start taking orders from us!"

"Guards!" Seavil commanded. "Nobody talks to the Mighty Seavil that way. Just for that you're getting one of my smaller cells."

"Ready guys?" Daniel yelled. "Let's show Seavil some manners."

Nikki and Scuba were indeed ready. Earlier they packed their ears with seaweed to block out Daniel's screech. To be on the safe side, Nikki still covered her ears. Before the seathons could reach any of them, Daniel sent out his sonic screech, knocking out the pathetic snakes.

Seavil roared with laughter, "You really thought your pitiful little squeal would work on someone as mighty as I? You're not as impressive as I thought."

"You're probably right, Your Majesty," Daniel snickered. "Mind if I give it another try?"

"I admire your boldness, little one. If you must, give me your best shot, or should I say shout," Seavil smiled. "Go ahead, knock yourself out."

"I'm not the one going to be knocked out, oh Great One," Daniel laughed.

Seavil did not realize what had just happened. With Daniel's first screech he not only knocked out the seathons, he also triggered Scuba's modified crown. A giant clam shell, one on each side of the crown, sprang forth behind Seavil's ears.

"I guess it's you that's not so impressive. Say goodnight, snake eyes," Daniel barked.

Daniel dug deep and let rip the loudest screech ever, which was amplified by the clam shells, more than enough to stun and knock out Seavil, bringing him crashing atop his mounds of glistening treasure.

Scuba shrugged with a smile, his back up plan had worked.

"You two all right?" Daniel asked as he received two enthusiastic thumbs up signs. "Okay, go ahead and get sleepy head ready for the trip. I'll take care of the seathons and the prisoners."

Daniel released all the prisoners, after first releasing his father.

"I'm so proud of you, son," his dad said as he proudly hugged Daniel. "Now let's go help the Princess."

"No Dad," Daniel corrected, "your place is at home with mom. I have enough help here to save the Princess."

"Your mother is worried about you, she wanted to come along, but..."

Daniel stopped his dad. "It's all right Dad. Go home. Tell mom everything is fine and tell the coach I'll be back in time for that last game."

"All right, but be careful Daniel," his dad said as he turned to go.

"Nikki! Scuba! Is everything ready to go?" Daniel asked.

"Everything's ready," Nikki smiled.

Daniel whispered into Seavil's ear, "Wake up sleepy head. Come on big guy, we're taking a trip."

"Taking a trip, are we? Got a slight headache, do I? Decided to help save the Princess, did I?" Seavil dribbled as he woke up.

Nikki laughed, "You got ole snake eyes talking like his goofy cousins."

"He'll be all right," Daniel said as he pulled on the reigns of Seavil's new harness. "Now, let's go save ourselves a princess!"

CHAPTER 11

SEAVIL'S SPEED MADE UP FOR LOST TIME, but it looked like it wasn't good enough. As the heroes reached the Ivory Coast, they ran straight into the expedition, Ivory Princess and all.

"Hold up Seavil," Daniel yelled, pulling back on the reigns.

"Looks like they were faster than I thought. Nikki, do me a favor. Take some rocks and see if you can jam them into the boat's propellers. That should slow them down a bit."

"You got it, Captain," Nikki joked as she raced away.

"Excuse me guys, will ya? Like to go and rest awhile, would I?" Seavil begged.

"Get as much rest as you can because I might need you in awhile," Daniel said as Seavil glided to the ocean's floor.

Suddenly, Daniel noticed that Nikki had been pulled onto the boat, but not until after she completed her task of jamming the propellers.

"Oh great," Daniel sighed, "here we go again. Could things get any worse?"

"Dan," Scuba yelled, "I think that's worse," he said as he pointed. "SSSSharks!"

They both turned to swim away but instead ran right into a mountainous rock, blocking their escape route. Before they could find a way around, the group of sharks were upon them.

Daniel searched for one of his screeches, but could not find one. He was scared screechless. Just as the sharks were about to attack, a familiar face popped out from behind.

"Hi guys," Karky smiled. "Sorry for the scare. I had to make sure it was you Daniel."

"Who are you?" Scuba asked.

"Karky, the world's only vegetarian shark, at your service. These are my brothers. I told them what you did Daniel, and although they're not too keen on the vegetarian part, they agreed to give us a hand."

"Great! This is Scuba the sea squirrel." Daniel introduced as he explained what had happened so far.

"They have my buddy Nikki up there," Karky growled.

"Don't worry Dan, we'll get her back, but first let's get the Princess out of here."

The sharks went right to work using their razor sharp teeth to cut through the harness holding the Princess.

"Scuba," Daniel yelled, "Get the Princess to safety. We will take care of the expedition!"

When they noticed the Princess had escaped, diver after diver jumped into the water. They tried to swim after the Princess, but had their hands full with the sharks. A couple of the divers freed the jammed propeller and it started to spin again. Daniel and his friends held their own, as spears and harpoons whizzed by.

They successfully fought off the ever increasing number of divers by ripping off their face masks and chewing through their air hoses.

Everything was going the rescuer's way until Daniel found himself in another little jam. A group of divers, spear guns in hand, cornered him in front of the ship's propeller. They pressed on, driving Daniel closer and closer to the spinning propeller. He had nowhere to turn.

"Why not?" Daniel thought as he once more sent out his sonic screech, cracking the advancing divers' masks and letting in the ocean's water. The divers scrambled to the surface.

Daniel took this chance to thank his shark friends and inform them of his next move. "Karky, I can't thank you all enough, but as soon as those divers regroup they will be back and in greater numbers. I've got an idea that will take care of this expedition. There's no sense in any of you guys getting hurt. Just do me one more favor, go help Scuba watch over the Princess. I'll catch up with you later."

With that, they parted.

Next, Daniel woke Seavil and explained what he had in mind.

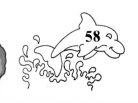

CHAPTER 12

AS THE DIVERS WERE ABOUT TO DIVE BACK in the water, Daniel surfaced, belly down, appearing to float on the water. Smiling, with fins under his chin, Daniel addressed the astonished crew. "Excuse me gentlemen, there seems to be a slight misunderstanding.

I understand your expedition was very exhausting and costly, but I am prepared to reimburse you," Daniel said and tossed a sack of treasure onto the boat. "Some of us dolphins love being with people, but there are some that just can't be taken from their home, like the Ivory Princess. She will surely perish away from her waters. Please understand this. Just take the treasure and release Nikki. Then, we can all reward from this little mishap."

The captain spoke up, "How are you floating like that?"

Daniel answered, "The sea holds many mysteries and secrets, some you weren't meant to understand. Now, please release my friend and go."

"How 'bout this?" the captain sneered. "We take the money, and when you return the white dolphin we'll think about returning the swimming rodent."

"Captain, I tried to work things out," Daniel replied. "Don't forget to tell your friends about what you've seen here today, in case they get any crazy ideas."

Daniel then tapped the water underneath him. Slowly, the crew realized Daniel was being supported by another sea creature. Seavil raised his head out of the water, and snarled at the stubborn captain and crew. He roared loudly, turning the crews' faces a ghostly white.

The men completely forgot about Nikki as she jumped into the sea. Before she hit the water, the captain and crew were well on their way back to shore.

Nikki cheered and gave Seavil a high five. "Feels nice being a good guy, huh Seavil?"

"Hop on Nik, let's go see if the Princess is all right."

Seavil really did feel good as he carried his newly acquired friends back to the ocean's depth.

CHAPTER 13

DANIEL, NIKKI AND SEAVIL FOUND everyone safely hidden in the dreary remains of a decaying shipwreck.

"It's all right everyone. The expedition is gone and I don't think they'll be back," Daniel reassured.

Everyone cheered!

"Are you all right, Princess?" Daniel asked.

"I'm fine Daniel, thanks to you and your friends. Thank you very much," the white dolphin said. "You are all very brave and should be proud of yourselves."

They were indeed very proud as they beamed with joy and congratulated each other. Nikki probably smiled the most, almost breaking out in laughter as she looked over and saw Karky chewing on some seaweed. She raced over and gave her new friend a big hug.

While everyone celebrated, the white dolphin pulled Daniel aside and spoke to him. "I appreciate your understanding the uniqueness of the Ivory Dolphin. Your courage has saved us from becoming extinct."

The Ivory Dolphin continued,

62

"You must understand that I, like yourself, would have done anything to keep the Ivory Dolphin from ever fading away."

"I don't understand," Daniel said.

The white dolphin guided Daniel to a hidden cavern beneath the sunken ship, and paused in front of the entrance.

"Come on out honey, the humans are gone," the Ivory Dolphin called. "I'm the Ivory Queen, Daniel. This is my daughter, Crystal, the real Ivory Princess."

Daniel's eyes sparkled as the Ivory Princess, glowing with beauty, emerged from the cave.

"I had to pretend to be the Princess to protect her." The Ivory Queen continued, "I feared nobody would come to help. I had to come up with a plan. If I had been captured it would not have mattered, for the Princess could still live a long life, ensuring the survival of her and our race."

"You, too, are a very brave dolphin, My Lady," Daniel proclaimed. "I am honored to have helped save two very special ladies. Now if you'll excuse me, I have to go help my friends at home win a championship."

"If you don't mind," the Queen requested, "the Princess and I would love to watch you play in the championship."

Daniel was shocked. What a thrill to have them both at the game. He blushed and replied happily, "I'd be honored!"

CHAPTER 14

THE GAME WAS JUST ABOUT OVER, THE championship on the line, as Daniel marched to the plate one more time. Only this Daniel was different. He was more confident.

It was the bottom of the ninth, two outs, two dolphins on base, and down two runs.

"Go get 'em Dan. Show 'em how it's done," the coach winked.

"Reach for the stars," Daniel said to himself, ignoring the snickering from the Stingers bench. Daniel looked toward his family and friends then toward the Stingers dugout, flashed them a thumbs up and turned toward the pitcher. He prepared himself as he watched the first pitch zip right by him.

"Strike one!" the umpire shouted.

Daniel couldn't believe it. This pitcher wasn't going to give this one up easily.

"Come on Daniel," he said to himself, "all you need is a single to tie this one up."

Daniel glanced over the pitcher's shoulder and smiled as he saw his enormous friend, Seavil, watching from outside the stadium, waving a Dolphin's banner.

"Knock yourself out, kid!" Seavil shouted, looking in.

Daniel chuckled, readied himself and swung at the lightning fast pitch that whizzed by his bat.

"Strike two!" the umpire shouted.

66

"Well, this is it," Daniel said to himself as he glanced over at the Stingers first baseman.

The Stinger sneered and winked at Daniel--the same Stinger that tripped him in the previous game. He was mocking Daniel. That's all Daniel needed as he readied himself one last time, choking up on his bat. He gave this swing everything he had and felt a feeling he had never felt before. No way was that hit going to be a single. The ball went sailing through the water, out of the park, and crashing into the Stingers name on the scoreboard, making it flicker and burn out.

Daniel beamed as he started his victory swim around the bases. Just as he reached first base, he put out his fin, as if to shake the first baseman's fin. When they were about to shake, Daniel reached up and tipped his hat to the cheering crowd. The two opposing teammates smiled at each other as Daniel continued around the bases. Daniel rounded third and smiled at his welcoming party at home plate.

"What a feeling," Daniel thought as he glanced up at the stars. He hoped it would never end, racing toward his cheering family and friends and especially the Ivory Princess.

68

Additional copies of
DANIEL AND THE IVORY PRINCESS
by Kevin Martin
may be ordered by sending a check or
money order for $17.95 postpaid for
each copy to:

Distinctive Publishing Corp.
P.O. Box 17868
Plantation, FL 33318-7868
800-683-3722

Quantity discounts are also available
from the publisher.

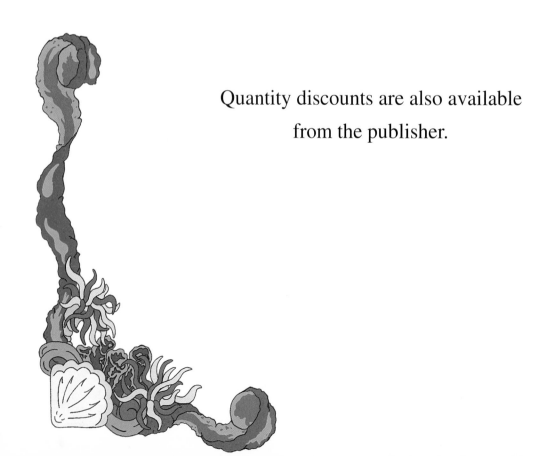